To Emma, sister of my heart and kindred spirit
And to Julie, for singing the soundtrack of my childhood
—JH

This book is dedicated to my cousin Alice,
with whom I've spent many childhood afternoons listening to Julie's songs,
watching *Mary Poppins* and living a lot of magical adventures
—IU

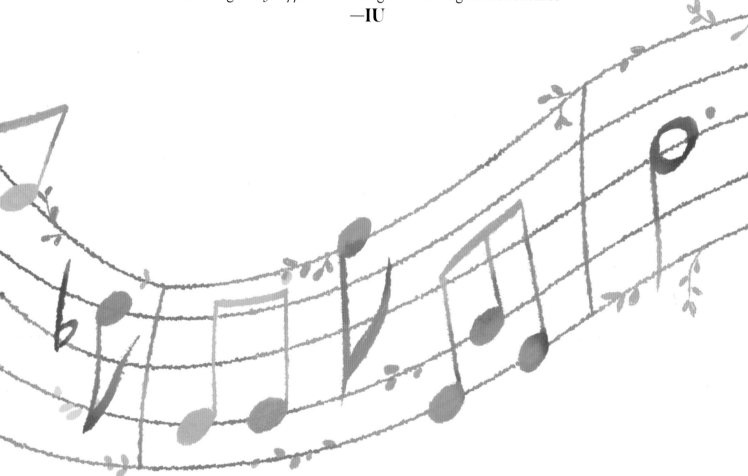

 little bee books

New York, NY
Text copyright © 2023 by Julie Hedlund
Illustrations copyright © 2023 by Ilaria Urbinati
All rights reserved, including the right of reproduction in whole or in part in any form.
Manufactured in China RRD 0523
First Edition
1 3 5 7 9 10 8 6 4 2
Library of Congress Cataloging-in-Publication Data is available upon request.
ISBN 978-1-4998-1379-1 | littlebeebooks.com
For more information about special discounts on bulk purchases,
please contact Little Bee Books at sales@littlebeebooks.com.

FSC
www.fsc.org
MIX
Paper | Supporting
responsible forestry
FSC® C144853

Song after Song

The Musical Life of Julie Andrews

written by
Julie Hedlund

illustrated by
Ilaria Urbinati

little bee books

Julia Elizabeth Wells was born into a melody—
her childhood attuned to the timbre
of her tiny English village where she heard music

in the rhythm of the river,

in the whistle of the wind,

in the symphony of songbirds.

Music surrounded her at home too.
Julia's mother played piano,
a talent that often took her to faraway places,
so it was her father who made their house a home.

He whistled, hummed, and sang as he cooked, cleaned,
and cared for Julia and her brother, Johnny.
At bedtime, he read stories and recited poetry,
and his voice wrapped around the house like a hug.

But in the midst of the Blitz of World War II,
Julia's mother moved to London
with a singer named Ted Andrews.

She sent for Julia to live with them.

Stuck in the sooty city of London, Julia longed for home.
Ted was unfamiliar to her, and no substitute for her father.
But her mother asked her to call him "Pop"
and changed Julia's name to Julie Andrews.

Julie struggled to find harmony in her new life.
Instead of a steady rhythm, Julie heard
the staccato sound of bombs dropping on the streets,
forcing her to flee with her mother and Ted
to the shelter of a nearby Underground station.

As people cooked on portable stoves, sipped tea,
and huddled together, Ted strummed his guitar and sang.
Sharing music with her sheltering neighbors comforted Julie
and kept her mind off the danger.

Soon Julie's school closed due to the war.
To keep her busy, Ted taught her to sing.

They were all astonished to discover
that from this sprite of a girl sprang a voice
as pure and clear as a cloudless summer sky.

Julie practiced singing every day as she was told,
but she found no joy in her gift.

Note after note, Julie suffered through her scales
while missing her father's warmth and love.

Fortunately, Ted turned over her vocal training
to famed singer and teacher Madame Lilian Stiles-Allen.
Madame combined rigorous instruction
with kindness and affection.

She taught Julie to imagine placing
each note right next to the previous one,
like a beautiful string of pearls.

Under Madame's tutelage, Julie found joy in music. Singing enabled her to express all the emotions she normally kept inside. She poured her heart into her practice and sometimes shed tears while singing sad songs. Madame told her never to be embarrassed when moved by music.

"It shows that you are a sensitive human being . . . capable of much feeling."

For the first time, Julie understood
that her voice was not just her gift,
but one she could share with others.

With her newfound purpose behind the practice,
Julie was filled with gratitude for her voice.
And as her voice grew in strength, so too did her courage.

Shortly after the war ended,
and right before her tenth birthday,
Julie stepped onto a stage, climbed onto a crate,
and sang "Come to the Fair" with Ted.

Julie's voice rose to the rafters
as her mother's fingers flew across the piano.
When the audience erupted into applause,
she basked in the warm spotlight.

The crowds loved Julie and launched her into early stardom. She traveled up and down England, and her voice filled theaters and concert halls while the accolades of audiences filled her heart.

At first, her name appeared at the bottom of the programs of her performances.

But over the next two years, Julie Andrews rose to the top.

With that rise came responsibility.
Singing could not be just for joy.
The money she earned supported
her family and paid for their new home.

She vowed to work as hard as she could for as long as she could.

Measure after measure, Julie pressed on with her singing practice and her studies. For months, she managed near-nightly performances in far-flung places. She did not falter.

In between her trips, Julie's spirits
were buoyed with visits to her father.

At the age of thirteen, Julie concluded her first
year-long variety show, *Starlight Roof*.
She worried about what would come next for her.

The answer came quickly in the form of
an invitation—a command—to sing at
the upcoming *Royal Variety Performance*.

This annual event drew the best talent across Britain,
with the Queen of England in attendance.

Julie wanted to sing so well that the audience would be left spellbound.

On the evening of the performance, Julie gathered her courage,
stepped into the spotlight, and lifted her voice.
Her string-of-pearl song cascaded over the crowd

like the rhythm of a river,

the whistle of the wind,

the sweetest symphony
of a birdsong.

All underscored by the hum of her father's love.

Julie finished to a crescendo of applause,
led by the Queen herself.

Song after song, Julie captivated audiences
onstage and onscreen—as Eliza Doolittle,
Mary Poppins, Maria von Trapp, and many more roles.

Julie's millions of fans found hope, comfort, and courage in her characters. Her performances allowed them, at least for a short time, to transcend their daily troubles.
Even after she stopped singing, Julie used her voice to bring people joy, especially children.

Stage after stage,

Julie brought stories to life for young people.

Page after page, Julie penned poems and books for children featuring tractors and trucks, fairy princesses, and of course—music.

Julie Andrews, born into a melody in a tiny English village,
wrapped her voice around the world like a hug.

Author's Note

Like many girls of my generation, I grew up loving Julie Andrews as Mary Poppins and Fraulein Maria. Every year, during my family's spring visit to my grandparent's house, I sat riveted in front of the tiny kitchen television, watching Julie spin across the Alpine Hills singing, *The Sound of Music*. After my Grandpa finished watching the evening news, the whole family would gather to watch the rest of the movie on the "big" TV.

When I learned years later that Julie had lost her singing voice after a throat surgery, I was devastated. At the time, I was beginning my own career and working on finding my way in the world, my own voice. I couldn't imagine the world deprived of Julie's.

Luckily, Julie began using her voice in a new way—writing children's books. I did the same and my path crossed that of Julie's daughter, Emma Walton Hamilton, with whom Julie had written more than two dozen books.

Emma and I formed a fast friendship that has deepened into something close to sisterhood. Sitting on her patio one evening, I wondered aloud about the likelihood of a girl from a small town in Northern Michigan becoming great friends with a girl who grew up between New York and Los Angeles as the daughter of a mega-star. Emma said, "We were raised with the same values."

That simple comment led me to look at Julie's own childhood more closely, and when I told Emma I wanted to use my voice to tell her mom's story to today's children, she gave me her blessing, as did Julie Andrews herself.

Julie Andrews Timeline

1935: Julie Andrews is born on October 1 in Walton-on-Thames, Surrey, England

1938: Brother John "Johnny" Wells is born in June.

1939: World War II begins in Europe in September.

1940: Blitzkrieg begins in Britain. Julie sent to London to live with her mother and Ted "Pop" Andrews.

1942: Brother Donald Andrews is born in July.

1943: Ted Andrews begins giving Julie singing lessons.

1944: Julie's father, Ted Wells, marries Winifred "Win" Maud Hyde. Madame Lilian Stiles-Allen takes over Julie's singing lessons.

1945: WWII ends. Julie sings onstage for the first time—a duet with Pop called "Come to the Fair." Win Wells gives birth to Julie's sister, Celia.

1946: Julie regularly joins her mother and Pop's traveling vaudeville act. She makes her radio debut on a BBC Variety Show. Brother Christopher Andrews is born in May.

1947: Makes her top billing stage debut in a variety show called *Starlight Roof* at the London Hippodrome Theater.

1948: Sings "Polonaise" as a solo at the *Royal Variety Performance* at the London Palladium Theater, then leads the entire company in "God Save the King."

1956: Makes Broadway debut as Eliza Doolittle in *My Fair Lady*.

1959: Julie marries Tony Walton, a set and costume designer also from Walton-on-Thames, in May.

1960: Stars on Broadway as Queen Guinevere in *Camelot*.

1962: Daughter Emma Katherine is born.

1964: Julie plays title role in the Walt Disney film, *Mary Poppins*.

1965: Wins the Academy Award for Best Actress and the Golden Globe award for Best Actress – Motion Picture Comedy or Musical for her role in *Mary Poppins*. Julie and her *Mary Poppins* costars also win the GRAMMY Award for Best Album for Children. That same year, she also stars in *The Sound of Music* as Maria von Trapp.

1966: Wins the Golden Globe award for Best Actress – Motion Picture.

1968: Julie and Tony divorce.

1969: Julie marries American filmmaker Blake Edwards on November 12.

1971: *Mandy*, Julie's first book for children, is published.

1974: *The Last of the Really Great Whangdoodles* is published.

1979: Receives a star on the Hollywood Hall of Fame.

1982: Stars in a dual role as Victoria Grant and Count Victor Grezhinski in *Victor/Victoria*. Receives Golden Globe award for Best Actress – Motion Picture for her performance.

1997: Loses her singing voice after a failed throat surgery.

2000: Made Dame Commander of the British Empire by Queen Elizabeth II.

2000: *Dumpy the Dump Truck*, co-written with daughter Emma Walton Hamilton, is published.

2001: Stars as Queen Clarisse Rinaldi of Genovia in *The Princess Diaries*.

2007: Receives a Life Achievement Award from the Screen Actors Guild.

2008: *Home: A Memoir of My Early Years* is published.

2010: *The Very Fairy Princess*, first book in a series, co-written with daughter Emma, is a #1 *New York Times* bestselling book.

2011: Wins a GRAMMY Lifetime Achievement Award.

2017: Season 1 of *Julie's Greenroom*, a Netflix original series teaching preschoolers about the arts, is released.

2019: *Home Work: A Memoir of My Hollywood Years*, coauthored with Emma, is a #1 *New York Times* bestseller.

2020: *Julie's Library Show* podcast is launched.

2022: Receives American Film Institute Lifetime Achievement Award.

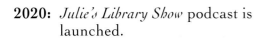
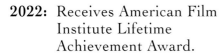